ISBN- 10 1500449512

ISBN- 13 9781500499513

# More Than One Way To Be Okay

Developing Cognitive Flexibility With Children

Written by Ronit Gross, LCSW-R
Illustrated by Izzy Bean

Dedicated to

Safira & Jesse

Annie was a lively and imaginative little girl. She could read and solve all sorts of math problems. She remembered poems and songs after hearing them only one time. She loved to draw and made all kinds of art projects.

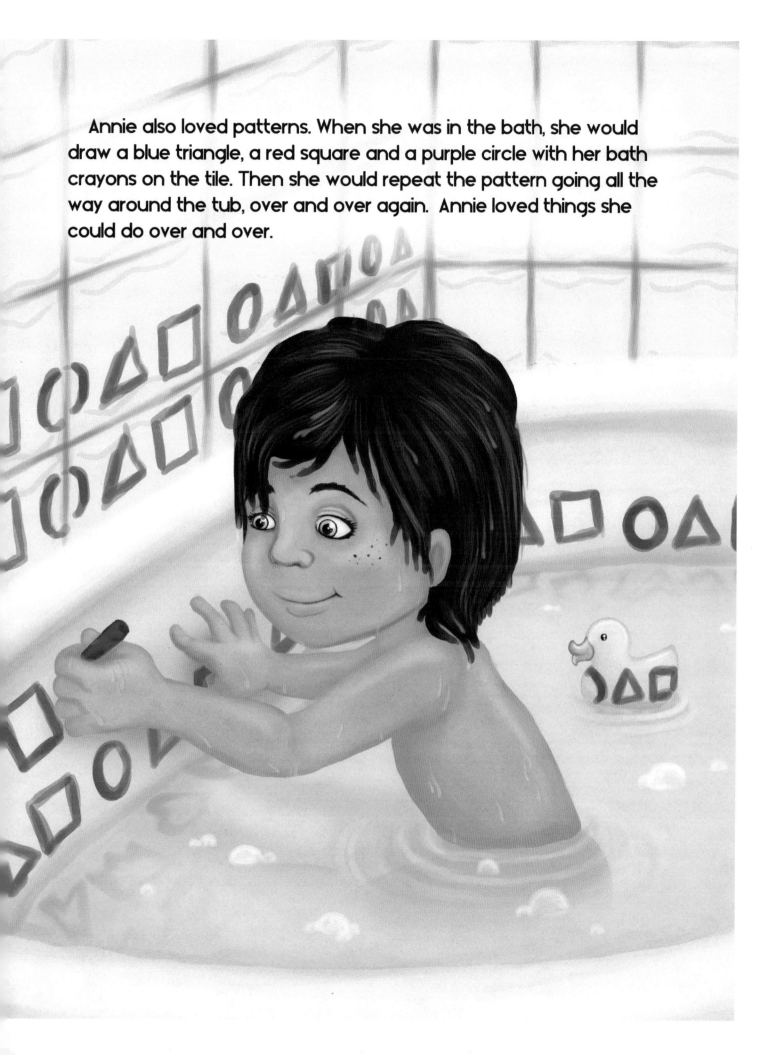

Annie also loved patterns. When she was in the bath, she would draw a blue triangle, a red square and a purple circle with her bath crayons on the tile. Then she would repeat the pattern going all the way around the tub, over and over again. Annie loved things she could do over and over.

Like her bedtime routine. Annie liked a story, a song and then she liked her hugs and kisses. In that order. Her books were lined up in the order she wanted them read and she had a list of songs in her head that were also in the order she wanted them sung.

She was very certain that her blanket needed to look a particular way, halfway down the bed and folded over at the end for her to feel comfortable.

One night Annie went to pick out her favorite fairy book to read,
the very next one that she knew was in her pattern.
"OH NO!!!" She screamed. "OH NO THIS IS TERRIBLE!"

"What is it?" Her mom asked.

"I brought my fairy book to school this morning and I left it there!" Annie cried. "It was the next one in my book pattern!" Annie screamed and wailed for more than an hour. She couldn't follow her pattern! She felt like her whole world was becoming one big, huge mess and that nothing would ever feel right. Not ever again.

Annie's mother was quiet while she cried. Annie's sobs became softer until at last they stopped completely. Slowly, Annie began to take some breaths. Her mother smiled kindly at her.

"Sometimes life doesn't work out in certain orders and patterns" she said.

"But that makes me sad!" Annie began to cry again.

"That's okay. All people feel sad sometimes and other feelings too like worried or angry. Feelings are a part of being a person and they come and go. Would you like to hear a story about a turtle named Dave who had a lot of the same feelings that you do?"

Annie nodded. She wasn't ready to feel all the way better but she was trying to listen.

Her mother began.

"Once upon a time there was a little turtle named Dave. Dave loved to build things. He built forts with blankets and pillows. He built cars with toilet paper roll wheels that could really move.

Sometimes he built for fun and sometimes he built when he was feeling sad, angry or worried and the building would help him feel better. But sometimes, Dave couldn't feel better quickly enough and he didn't like that. He wondered if there was a way to escape from painful feelings altogether.

One day, Dave was sitting in his house when he thought of a wild idea.

"This is a wild idea" said Dave. Dave sawed and hammered. He glued and stapled. He sanded and painted. And at the end of a week, Dave had built his idea. It was a giant robot! Dave called his robot Feelin' Good Fun Guy.

Dave pretended Feelin' Good Fun Guy could walk when Dave pressed the WALK button on his remote control. And using his own voice, Dave pretended his robot could talk when he pressed the TALK button. And Dave made sure that Feelin' Good Fun Guy always had ideas about what would make Dave feel better.

At first, he made Dave laugh with all his silly games.

FEELIN'
GOOD

"Stand on your head and your stomach won't hurt" he would say when Dave pressed TALK. And Dave would laugh and stand on his head. It wasn't really true that being upside down would stop his tummy from hurting if he had a tummy ache but it was fun to pretend.

But as time went on, Feelin' Good Fun Guy was beginning to feel less and less good. He would tell Dave, "If You Don't Eat Your Fruit First, It Won't Taste Good" or "If You Don't Count To Ten Three Times, You'll Feel Sad".

Soon Feelin' Good Fun Guy had rules for EVERYTHING like which books Dave had to read at bedtime and what songs had to be sung in which order.

Dave became more worried and frustrated than ever. He forgot that he was the one who had built his robot. He forgot that he could turn his robot off. He began to believe Feelin' Good Fun Guy's words even though Dave was the one who made up the words in the first place.

It was so strange. Dave had built his robot so that he could feel better but instead he was feeling worse. It felt like Feelin' Good Fun Guy had become the boss of Dave.

Annie was listening to the story closely.

"I don't like Feelin' Good Fun Guy" she said. "If I was Dave, I would smash him to pieces."

"I can understand that" her mother said. "It seems like Feelin' Good Fun Guy was trying to protect Dave from his feelings because he didn't know that feelings, even the hard ones are safe to have."

Annie looked down.

"You know those things Dave's robot said? Sometimes I say those same things to myself."

"Like what?" Her mother asked.

"Like I tell myself that my books have to be in a certain order or I won't have any fun reading them. Or my songs have to follow my song pattern or I won't like hearing them and I won't be able to feel peaceful. Sometimes I tell my friends that they have to do things my way even when they don't want to. Sometimes they don't want to play with me after that. Those are the times when I let *my* robot make the decisions."

"Hmm" said her mother. "I see."
Annie looked at her mother.
"I don't want those kinds of thoughts to be in charge of me anymore Mommy."

Her mother hugged her.

"You know, a few minutes ago you were so miserable about leaving your book and now you seem much calmer even though the book is still at school. What's changed for you?"

"I took my mind off my book" Annie said. "I listened to your story. When I heard about Feelin' Good Fun Guy's rules I reminded myself that I have other books I can read. I told myself there was more than one way to be okay. Then I felt better."

And Annie realized she was feeling much better... even without her fairy book.

"I'm still going to try and remember to bring the book home tomorrow" she said. "But I'm not going to let my thoughts boss me around. I'll tell my robot that if I do forget, I might be disappointed but I'll be ok."

"Wow" said Annie's mother. "Sounds like you're the one helping your thoughts now."

Annie smiled.
"No more Feelin' Good Fun Guy in charge!" she said.

And she meant it too.

# For Parents

The ability to be cognitively flexible is a skill developed over time, similar to reading, walking and potty training. Like these other skills, children develop cognitive flexibility differently and at different ages. Most children (and sometimes adults) experience their feelings with a great deal of intensity, a tidal wave of emotion that blocks out any other perspective. Routines and patterns can be a normal and healthy way to manage these overwhelming feelings. Sometimes children can get stuck in these initially adaptive regiments, leaving both parents and children frustrated, angry and upset. It can be tempting to criticize what seems like unreasonable or "just plain stubborn" behavior but similar to learning to read or potty training, emotional education requires a calm and focused approach.

# Some Tips:

1. Wait until they've considerably calmed down. (Imagine trying to teach a screaming child how to read!) You can be calmly silent, walk away or if they are willing to listen you can try to describe what is happening. "Because I said we can't have ice cream today you feel as though you'll never be happy again."
Try to present the same kind of presence and thoughtfulness you wish your child would have.

2. Explore other options ie: "Do you want to play with your Legos instead?" "Should we choose another book?" "Would you like to listen to some music?" If they are unable to hear, you can just sit with them quietly, leave if your presence seems to exacerbate your child's behavior and if it seems to help, add simple statements. "This is really hard for you, I hear that."

3. When they are interested, tell them their story. "Do you want to hear your ice cream story?" Include how sad, angry or worried they had felt and how they had believed that "getting the ice cream" was the only solution to feeling better. Gently explore the differences between disappointment and disaster. Describe how, as time passed, they became otherwise involved and engaged in pleasurable activities and feelings once more. Remind them that feelings come and go. With compassion, share that there's more than one way to be okay.

4. Sometimes, children can get stuck in their perspective and what they see as their "need". They are unable to take in the experience or the response of another. This can result in repetitive asking for the same thing, even after a caregiver has said "no". One method of addressing this is to ask your child "What would happen if the answer is no?" Or "How would you handle it if the answer is no?" Initially a child might say "then I'll scream" or "I'll hate you". You can respond "That's understandable and if that's what you need to do/ how you feel that's okay. This will pass." Talking about the processing of a "no" instead of focusing on the child's specific desire can help break into a child's "tunnel vision."

If you are concerned about your child's behavior or your own ability to parent a challenging child, seek help from a child psychologist or therapist or a child behavioral expert. Your primary care doctor or your child's pediatrician can refer you to someone appropriate.

Ronit Gross, LCSW-R is a psychotherapist living and working in Brooklyn, NY with her husband and two children. Along with the children, she and her husband have many opportunities to practice their own cognitive flexibility...

Izzy Bean graduated from the University of Bolton in Greater Manchester, UK with a 1st class degree in Illustration and animation in 2009. Since then, Izzy has been illustrating for children's authors in a fun and unique style.

www.izzybean.co.uk

Made in the USA
Lexington, KY
27 August 2015